Paul A. Chadbourne

The Hope of the Righteous

Discourses at the funerals of Prof. Albert Hopkins

Paul A. Chadbourne

The Hope of the Righteous
Discourses at the funerals of Prof. Albert Hopkins

ISBN/EAN: 9783337090609

Printed in Europe, USA, Canada, Australia, Japan

Cover: Foto ©Andreas Hilbeck / pixelio.de

More available books at **www.hansebooks.com**

THE

HOPE OF THE RIGHTEOUS

DISCOURSES AT THE FUNERALS OF

PROF. ALBERT HOPKINS, REV. DR. NAHUM GALE

AND

REV. DR. N. H. GRIFFIN

BY

P. A. CHADBOURNE

PRESIDENT OF WILLIAMS COLLEGE

NEW YORK

G. P. PUTNAM'S SONS

182 FIFTH AVENUE

1877

CONTENTS.

PERSONAL.

THERE are but few men who have reached the age of fifty years, who do not find themselves surviving the large portion of those friends to whom they early looked for sympathy and counsel. Those who stand almost alone in their generation, as one friend after another has weakened in the way, know how sad this loneliness at times becomes, and also what a precious treasure they possess in the memory of those whose friendship, free from selfishness and weakness, was a constant benefit and joy. When sorrow for the loss of such friends is mellowed by time, as the rough outlines of ravine and cliff are softened by vines and flowers, it is pleasant in thought to surround ourselves with those who are gone, whose lives were a blessing to us while they remained, and the memory of whom brings nothing but pleasant pictures to our view.

Among the many friends whose memory I have cause to cherish, the three whose names

are here joined together, were those whose remembrance will ever be a source of the purest
pleasure, as, in life, they were among those
who could be counted upon as kind and true
in all the varied relations in which we were
placed together. A life-long sorrow must follow the loss of such friends ; but with that
sorrow are mingled blessings, which the friendship of such men can alone bring.

It is one of the most pleasant things in my
life, that these three men with whom I had
been so long associated in various ways—as
pupil, colleague, and friend—should in their
last moments turn their thoughts to me —
though two of them were far from me—and
request that I should speak the last words for
them to their kindred and friends. To have
the confidence and love of such men to the
last after so many years, and to know by such
proofs that you were present in their thoughts,
as one who understood them, as one to be
trusted in things most sacred to them and those
whom they loved, is a comfort that outweighs
a thousand harsh judgments of those who are
hurrying selfishly through the world disturbed
by the perplexities of daily life.

The discourses are printed as they were delivered, excepting the slight changes absolutely required for the press, though from the circumstances of the case, in respect to the first two, there were but a few hours for their preparation. In reference to the third, Dr. Griffin specially requested that no formal discourse should be pronounced. The few remarks were written out from the scanty notes prepared at the time.

If any apology is required for the publication of discourses such as these, delivered under so unfavorable conditions for full elaboration, it is found in the desire of some who remember with affection these friends who are gone, to preserve the words spoken of them in compliance with their own last request. I desire also to put on record my estimate of these men, to whom I personally and the College over which I have been called to preside, owe so much.

From the time of my entering Williams College, in 1845, till Professor Hopkins' death in 1872, our relations were as intimate and confidential as it seems possible they could be between persons situated as we were. As student under his instruction, as his colleague in college for many years, as member of his family, and co-worker with him in many undertakings, I have now, and shall ever retain, the most delightful recollections of his unvarying kindness and pure Christian life. His love of nature, his fervid religious character, by which he moved among us almost with the power of a prophet of old, his genial humor that never weakened the influence of his religious life, and his active sympathy with everything that pertained to his friends, made him one of the most pleasant companions and valued associates that it could fall to the lot of any man to possess. His whole life is like a pleasant picture where the grandeur of mountain scenery is combined with the beauty of unruffled lake and cultivated vale ; his memory, like precious ointment poured out.

With Dr. Gale, I became acquainted at East Windsor Hill Seminary, in 1851. That acquaintance continued and became more intimate as we labored together for the College, one as trustee and the other as officer. And, especially, during my Presidency, the counsel and sympathy of Dr. Gale were prompt and hearty. Though not loving controversy, he did not shrink from responsibility ; and his aid and encouragement were ready at any moment when needed. The words spoken by him, as he turned from me the last time on the Commencement stage, were such as he might have spoken had he known they were to be his last. His wise counsel, faithful labor, and cheerful words will long be remembered by those who have been associated with him in official duties.

Dr. Griffin came into the College as Professor, in 1846, at the beginning of my junior year. As instructor and pupil, as colleagues in college work, and as friends, our relations were intimate for the rest of his life. And it was by his dying bed alone of the three, that I had the privilege of sitting to speak with him of our past days, and to talk of the future of the two worlds. It was, indeed, a privilege to see how a good man can die ; with what courage one, who has shrunk from conflict all his days, can, when the time comes, meet every requirement of God's providence, even death itself.

Dr. Griffin was a most judicious counselor. If he ever erred, it was on the side of caution.

1*

But with all his natural caution, he never hesitated to recommend prompt action nor to assume responsibility where principle was involved.

In all questions relating to theology and philosophy, Dr. Griffin's learning and judgment were equaled by very few. As a critic in all the higher realm of learning and thought, his aid was eagerly sought by those who were laboring in the same fields. As a faithful laborer for the College in all his relations to it, he had no superior. There is but one verdict from all those capable of judging of his service. It awards him the praise of unwavering fidelity and untiring labor.

While these three men had strongly marked individuality, they were, as may readily be inferred, in many important respects alike. They were men of learning, of devoted piety, of irreproachable lives, of great usefulness ; and they were true in all trusts and in all the relations of life,—men to whom one would love to turn in confidence, when tempted to believe that all men are false. They were friends to each other; and it is one of the choicest blessings of my life that I have been able to reckon

them among my friends ; one of the rich trea-
sures of memory which advancing life has
brought, that in the long intercourse with all
these men, there is not a single cloud or
shadow in the bright picture of the past, which
now alone is left.

Their places will be filled in the work of
life. The places in the college and pulpit may
be made good by those who are called to the
work which they have left, but the places
which they have left vacant in the hearts of
their friends will remain unfilled.

P. A. C.

Williams College, 1877.

PROFESSOR HOPKINS.

THE Bible abounds with descriptions of holy
men, and with symbols which typify the character and the blessedness of the servants of
God. In the hour of bereavement, we come to
the Bible for consolation, for words of comfort,
and for aid in appropriating to our good the
teachings of God's providence, as connected
with the life and the death of his children.

I have selected as appropriate to this oc-
casion, that portion of the Word of God, re-
corded in the xii. ch. of Daniel and 3d verse.

"AND THEY THAT BE WISE SHALL SHINE AS
THE BRIGHTNESS OF THE FIRMAMENT; AND THEY
THAT TURN MANY TO RIGHTEOUSNESS AS THE
STARS FOREVER AND EVER."

Amid the beauty and grandeur of this physical universe, the heavens have a glory of their
own; and they also give the only conditions
for revealing the beauty and grandeur of all
other objects. The firmament by day floods
the earth with light that beams directly from

the sun ; and from every silvery cloud and the blue enamel of the sky, come the softened rays of reflected light as a revealer and beautifier of every object that delights the eye. And in the darkness of night, the golden constellations illumine the heavens with the thousand stars that for ages have delighted the shepherd on the plain, the mariner on the deep, and every thoughtful observer of these heavenly bodies, as they move along their pathway in the sky.

It is only by symbols drawn from the natural world, that the perfections and glories of the spiritual world can be illustrated ; and these symbols, we are assured, fall far short of the glories that shall be revealed. But in our text, the radiance of the firmament by day and the beauty of the starry sky are set forth as symbols of human character, as that character may be revealed in its glorified state in its eternal home.

" *And they that be wise shall shine as the brightness of the firmament ; and they that turn many to righteousness, as the stars, forever and ever.*"

The wisdom so often referred to in the Bible,

is distinguished from the wisdom of this world, as being the choice of spiritual good ; the good which God is ready to bestow for the blessedness of his rational creatures, and the glory of his own name. The wise, whose glory and excellence are symbolized by the effulgence of the heavens in their mid-day splendor, are those who have chosen God as their portion ; His Word as their guide of life ; His spirit as their light and comfort, and His work as the great aim and joy of their lives.

A life of wisdom in this spiritual sense, a life given to the upbuilding of Christ's kingdom in the hearts of men, gives to us the highest exhibition of human character of which it is possible for us to conceive. Such a character is the image of Christ, and carries with it something of the indescribable glory which belongs to the Son of God, and which he bestows upon those who have been transformed into his image. When we have looked upon the heavens, bathed in the flooding light of the sun, and upon the radiance of the unchanging stars, as they declare the glory of God and surpass all other manifestations of beauty, order, and grandeur in the physical universe,

we feel how inadequate this all is to set forth
the excellencies and majesty of one who has
overcome in the moral conflicts with self and
the world, and become a pillar in the temple of
our God.

What object in all the world of matter, what
star or sun, what order of constellations, can
compare with the beauty and the excellence, or
with the majesty of the moral and religious life
of him who has now passed from our midst!

Such a life calls for a more thorough analy-
sis, and a more worthy memorial than the trib-
ute which we pay in this hour of our grief,
while the chariot and horsemen seem yet in
sight, and his mantle waits for some Elisha,
who with his power and spirit shall go forth in
the work which for more than forty years he
has performed for this college, this town, and
the world.

From a life so rich, the few things that can
be said at this time can but suggest to those
who knew him best, the excellencies of character and the abundance of labors which must
to-day be passed unnoticed, while we consider
a few of those elements of power and distinguished services that make his name a light

and glory to this college, one of the lights of the religious world, and which enable us by the eye of faith to behold him among the redeemed, clothed with the brightness of the firmament, receiving that crown more enduring than the stars, reserved for all those that love the appearing of the Lord.

Professor Hopkins was no ordinary man, even when judged by the standards of this world. In the prime of his physical powers, few men surpassed him in all those elements of manly beauty that attract attention and indicate at once great physical and intellectual activity and strength. In later life, when age had whitened his locks, and moral conflicts and triumphs had deepened the lines upon his face, he stood before us a form of dignity and beauty, which no ideal of patriarch or prophet ever surpassed.

The strength and beauty of form were but symbols of those high intellectual and moral powers which he possessed. These powers of body and mind he dedicated to the service of God and the welfare of man wherever duty led, without regarding the great personal sacrifices which he was called upon to make.

For the office of Professor in college he had unusual qualifications, as is abundantly shown by his many years of successful labor, even when contending against difficulties that would have entirely unfitted ordinary men for college work.

If labor was needed to prepare means for the practical illustration of the subject in hand, that labor he gave even when care, and grief, and weariness of body would have been an abundant excuse for omitting the exercise or lightening the work. In the philosophical lecture room and in the astronomical observatory, his learning, and patience, and skill as an experimenter and observer, were equally apparent.

He went abroad before a steamer had crossed the ocean ; when foreign travel was not, as it is now, easy of accomplishment, and a mere matter of pleasure. He went to visit the men of science, observe the new methods and means for philosophical investigation, and to secure for the college the needful apparatus for scientific study. He built the first astronomical observatory ever built for purposes of instruction in connection with any college in this country, quarrying the stones with his own hands,—

aided by the students, who had caught something of his own enthusiastic and progressive spirit,—and contributing largely from his own means for its erection.

Although the demands upon his time and strength in after life, by the orderings of Providence, prevented him from carrying on those extensive observations for which his taste and skill as an observer fitted him, the observatory has been made as practical an agency in education, under his direction, as in any college in our land.

He was not only faithful in imparting all the instruction required by the college course, but he was ever ready to aid and encourage those who were willing to undertake the labor to observe and become proficient in work in his department not required in the class-room. Among the sweetest recollections of my student life, is now and will be while I live, the remembrance of the nights spent with him in that observatory. His voice will be heard by me, as I enter the transit room ; and the measured beats of the faithful clock will remind me of the days and scenes that are passed.

One of the last labors which he performed

after he was too weak to attend to its publica-
cation, was the preparation of a Treatise upon
Astronomy.

"THE MEMORIAL PROFESSORSHIP" of Astronomy will have new and precious memories
connected with it, while the college stands.

But it was not in his own department alone,
that Professor Hopkins was an educating
power in the college. He was a lover of
Natural History in all its departments, and by
his direct, and more still by his indirect influence, did he aid, during his whole life, in making the study of nature attractive and profitable
to the students of the college. In 1835, he
organized, and with the late Professor Emmons,
led the first scientific expedition ever sent out
from this college, and, so far as I know, the
first expedition of the kind ever sent out by
any college in this country. A vessel was
chartered and fitted up for the purpose, and
Professor and students undertook together
among the islands and along the shores of
the Gulf of St. Lawrence, the study of Natural
History, and the collection of specimens for the
college cabinet. Such expeditions are com-
paratively common now, when travel is easy,

and the necessity of field-work in Natural History, is well understood. But that such an expedition should have been planned in a college among the Berkshire Hills, and successfully carried out nearly forty years ago, when as yet it was necessary to travel a hundred miles to reach the railroad, shows that the organizer of the expedition was one of those minds that see in advance the demands of science, and have wisdom and energy enough to adopt the most efficient means for its advancement.

He was also in a great measure instrumental in carrying out the subsequent expeditions from the college ; and by his words of cheer, and his active participation in the meetings of the Society of Natural History, his influence was scarcely less than it would have been had he occupied the chair of Natural History in the college. His peculiar traits of mind enabled him to do far more in this incidental way, than ordinary men could possibly accomplish. He was a thorough lover of nature, and no object was too small or too common to be worthy of his attention. The crystal and the flower, though seen for the hundredth time, had as much interest for him as for his student com-

panion, who now looked upon it as a new re-
velation of the Creator's wisdom and skill.

This love for the beautiful in nature, was
more fully manifested, perhaps, in the perfec-
tion of his æsthetic judgment, which enabled
him to select at a glance the best point of a
landscape, and in that taste, which enabled him
to give new beauty whenever he had the means
of improvement.   Living all his life among the
varied beauties of Berkshire County, and for
the large portion of his life, in this valley, he
never wearied of seeking new combinations in
the landscape, and of encouraging by word and
act, every effort to add to the beauty of the
natural scenery.

The last day of his life, when the shadows
were lengthening, when the scenes of the eternal world were opening before him, and his
heart was going out for the spiritual welfare of
all around him, he found time to give minute
directions for the beautifying of the grounds of
the little chapel where he had spent so much
time and strength.   What must have been the
calmness of spirit, and what the estimate of
the element of beauty in its influence for moral
and religious good, which could have recalled

the thoughts of such a man to the beautifying of that glen, as he was closing his eyes upon brooks and flowers and landscapes of earth forever!

If we now pass from the consideration of those special traits of character which give success in the class-room and in the general work of a college officer, we shall find that all these were strengthened by his high qualities in social life. If there have been those who considered Professor Hopkins as severe and unsocial, they are those who have judged without acquaintance. No man ever enjoyed more fully all the pleasant relaxations of life. He was sure to become the joyous center of any social circle in which he moved ; and as he grew older, he daily became more genial, more companionable for youth, entering into all those plans which heighten the innocent enjoyments of life. Long will he be remembered for the enjoyment which his pure and happy nature gave to the young and old who have associated with him.

As a husband, giving years of tender care to an invalid wife—giving, without a murmur, the time and strength of the best years of his life, that might have given him a still higher name among scientific men—as a father, giving up his only son for the service of his country, and bowing with Christian resignation as that young life went out in the shock of battle ; as a friend, that never failed, as a companion giving delight to all associated with him, Professor Hopkins was a model man. He was wise in word and act, and he combined with wisdom those genial qualities that attract friends and do so much to heighten the enjoyment of daily life. In all the relations indicated, his character is beautiful, shining like the sunlight and stars, and his memory, to his friends, will be a precious legacy as they recall the pleasure which his friendship afforded, and mold their own lives by the example he has left.

But in considering all these characteristics, we have not reached the great element of power in his life, that which molded and controlled all his activities, that for which he will be longest remembered, through which he impressed upon the world an influence that will not be lost while suns and stars revolve, and which will insure to him the brightness of the firmament when the sun has paled and the stars no longer illume the sky.

Professor Hopkins was eminently a man of God. His conduct in every relation in life bore witness that he was worthy of this name ; but in the special works, which more distinctly mark the servant of Christ, he has been a wonder to those who have lived and labored with him.

The change in his views when he dedicated himself to God was sudden and radical ; and his whole life was daily molded by the power of the Gospel of Christ. This no one could doubt—no one ever did doubt. It was his intention to devote himself to the missionary work in foreign lands, but when the call was made from the college, he wisely accepted it as a call from God, to occupy a place where he has probably rendered more efficient aid to the missionary work than he could have rendered in any foreign field. How many devoted missionaries have gone out quickened by his Christian life, and rendered more efficient in their work through his instruction, his precepts, and example !

In another age and in different relations he

2

might have been a mystic ; but his active zeal
for the salvation of men left him no time for
mere speculation and dreams.   His was an
active Christian life.   He went out into the
highways and hedges, and wherever hearers
could be found, there he proclaimed the everlasting Gospel.   Upon these hills, in this
church, in the college, and wherever the providence of God called him, he proclaimed the
Word.   And in pungent, effective preaching,
and in certain forms of expository preaching,
he was unsurpassed.   Hundreds who have
listened to him, in times of revival, will bear
witness to that wondrous power of voice and
language that controlled and moved the whole
assembly as one man, that made the unseen
world a dread reality, thundering the terrors
of a broken law and revealing the infinite love
of a waiting Saviour.

With what vividness and beauty did Bible
scenes appear as, with magic power of poetic
language, he portrayed the deeds of the wor-
thies of Bible-history!   The stories of Abraham
and Jacob and Moses, of Elijah and David became a sacred drama, as these men of God
and the scenes in which they were actors

passed before us. But the great central figure
of the Bible was the central figure in all his
preaching. "Christ and him crucified" was
the great theme upon which he loved to dwell.
Christ was the captain under whose banner he
marched; Christ was the pilot in whom he
trusted when "waiting by the river." The
last time that I met him, he told me of his
thoughts in the night watches, and read to me
some of the sermons, in sentences, which were
repeated to us on the Sabbath, and that sermon, that with a polished crystal, as a symbol
of Christian life, he was preparing, like the
Apostle of old, to send as an epistle to his
church.*

In systematic labor for the promotion of
religion, he was a marked example of faithfulness. For forty years, the noon prayer-meeting has been sustained in this college ; of that
meeting Professor Hopkins has been the lead-
er. In days of weariness, even when borne
down with anxiety and labor and weakness,
how rarely has his place been vacant! Sometimes the room was thronged ; sometimes but
two or three met together in the Saviour's

---

* To the Church in " White Oaks."

name, but his zeal and faithfulness never wavered. As the word goes forth throughout this land and among the missionary stations in different parts of the world, that he has gone, there will be sorrow for the loss of a faithful instructor and Christian friend ; but of all the memories which this sad news will awaken, the scenes in the prayer-meeting and in the conference-room, will be most vividly recalled. They will be remembered as largely depending for their interest upon the constant, faithful labors of him whose work is now done.

But piety and zeal like his, could not be confined to college walls. This church and this whole community will bear witness to his unwearied labors, in former years, in the support of social meetings and in the public ministrations of the Word. You are ready to testify to his liberality and Christian love in coming to your aid, preaching and laboring without money and without price, for more than two years, that he might lighten your burdens in the building of this sanctuary, and thus secure to you the means of the permanent ministrations of the Gospel.

But before this, his heart went out to a more

destitute part of the town. And through his agency, the White Oaks Chapel was built ; and there he has labored and organized agencies for good, that are equal to the results of an ordinary lifetime, inaugurating a work that will bless this whole town, and be the means, through the grace of God, of bringing many to the knowledge of the truth, of making them stars in the crown of his rejoicing, adding to the brightness of that glory promised to those who turn many to righteousness.

Of him, it could be truly said for the forty-five years that he has moved among you in these varied relations in life, that he was instant in season and out of season, that he was ever, fervent in spirit, serving the Lord.

And happy, transcendently happy was the close of his life, in what God permitted him to see as the fruits of his labors, in what he was able to do for others, and in that faith and Christian hope by which he was sustained till the Master called.

That chamber of death was a fitting close to such a life. With powers of mind clear and comprehending every interest to the last, with fit words of comfort and instruction to those dear ones around him, to neighbors and friends, with messages of love to the absent, with calm trust in God, without a doubt or fear, his life went out, not in darkness, but in a radiance of heavenly light.

Was it an accidental thing, that the debt which he labored to remove from this church, should have been removed before he passed away? Was it a thing of accident, that as his eight years' work in the " White Oaks " was closing, the Spirit should be poured out there, and that he should be permitted in his sick-chamber to welcome young converts from the field of his labor? It may truly be said of him, that his last days were his best days. With so many tokens of divine favor, with all the surroundings of love and honor which the heart of man could desire, and with the hope of a glorious immortality, he has passed to his rest.

His work is done ; and we gather to-day in bereavement and sorrow. We weep for ourselves, and not for him.

"Servant of God, well done."

The voice which the Revelator heard from

heaven comes echoing to us, as we contemplate this Christian character, this life so abounding with fruit. *" Blessed are the dead which die in the Lord, from henceforth ; yea, saith the Spirit, that they may rest from their labors ; and their works do follow them."*

His toils and cares, and his labors of love for this college, this church, and this people, are ended. He walks by the river of life before the throne of God and the Lamb. He is gathered to the goodly company of patriarchs and prophets, who have triumphed through faith and have entered the holy city. But his name and his example remain to us, a precious legacy to this college and to this people.

To all the Faculty of this institution of which he was the senior member—the honored and the well-beloved—this is a day of sorrow and bereavement. His death, I would rather say his whole life, comes to admonish us of duty, to encourage us in faithful labor for the intellectual and religious welfare of the college, for which he so long labored, and to which his name will continue such a blessing. Many a heart will swell with a deeper love for the institution and with more earnest prayers for its success,

as the Alumni make their annual pilgrimage to
the place of his rest.

To the students of the college, there comes
a voice calling upon them to seek wisdom—not
the wisdom of this world which shall pass away,
but that wisdom which has guided this life so
beautiful in all its development, so transcendently beautiful in moral and religious perfections, that all the wisdom and philosophy of
this world can only wonder at and admire it.
Will they seek to be gathered with the wise,
who shall shine as the brightness of the firmament when the honors and distinctions of life
shall be forgotten ?

To this people, his labors of love, his words
of warning and instruction, and his godly life,
should speak to-day as with a voice from beyond the tide.   He has no new Gospel to proclaim, that he should return to repeat the messages with new sanctions and with more precious promises.   You know the words that he
would speak.   The cross of Christ was all his
trust, his glory in his days of strength, his support and comfort in the days of weakness.
Shall it be a mere passing incident to you, that
his last service in this church was to break the

bread and commemorate with you the dying love of Christ? that his last sermon in this pulpit, was from the words of God's ancient servant, " *Choose ye this day whom ye will serve* " ? As the beginning of that sermon was a call to you, so the close of it seemed to have prophetic reference to his own departure.

He spoke of the heavenly rest in these words : " For Joshua being a hundred and ten years old, there remained to him only a burying place on the hill of Gaash. But the choice involves more—for says the Apostle, ' If Joshua had given them rest, then would he not afterwards have spoken of another, saying, There remaineth therefore a rest for the people of God,' a rest from pain, from sorrow, and from sin.

> ' No chilling winds, no poisonous breath,
>   Can reach that healthful shore ;
>   Sickness and sorrow, pain and death
>   Are felt and feared no more.'

Let us labor, brethren, to enter into that rest." These were his last words from this pulpit. From that rest he speaks to-day. Shall his words to you in all his ministrations here be as good seed sown in good ground, or shall

2*

they find lodgment only among choking thorns and upon stony earth?

To the bereaved wife, whose privilege it was to aid in his works of love, and minister to his wants in the last days of his life; to the stricken brother now separated from the one whose name has so long been linked with his own, in the great work of life; to all these sorrowing friends, I would speak words of comfort. But what words can add to the consolations which such a life and such a death afford?

And how shall I speak words of comfort to others, when my own heart swells with grief as I remember my own bereavement? My elder brother, counselor, and friend is taken— a new sorrow has come to my heart, a new weight to the burden of my life. This college will seem strange; and one place in it will never be filled. These hills have a shadow of gloom upon them for some of us, that the thousand stars of night or the brightness of the sun can never wholly dispel. One saintly form will no more appear among us, one voice so pleasant to us all is hushed. These hills and grounds and the sanctuaries that he loved, will know him no more forever. We must walk our own paths without his words of counsel, bear our burdens without his generous aid.

But from among the shining throng, there seems to come a voice to comfort and sustain. We know that voice would proclaim the unchangeable love of God, the wisdom of His way. It would counsel us in this day of darkness, to lift our eyes to the light which God can give, and to hear the voice that comes from His providence and Word. Yes, Heavenly Father, we will listen to the voice which comes to us from the life and counsels of thy servant. We listen to the words of thy Son. We trust in Thy wisdom and love. Though clouds and darkness are round about Thee, righteousness and judgment are the habitation of Thy throne. To THEE we commit the interests of this people, to THEE we commit this college in this day of its bereavement. Cover it with the shadow of Thy wings, sanctify it by Thy grace, raise up in it multitudes who shall imitate him whom Thou hast called to his rest—a multitude who shall shine with him as the brightness of the firmament, and as the stars forever and ever.

AMEN.

REV. DR. GALE.

THERE are hours of brightness and beauty in the physical world, and days of gloom and darkness and storm. The evening sky is a revealer of worlds, that declare the glory of God, or it is covered with impenetrable cloud that gathers like a pall around the earth, and has in itself no apparent promise of life or blessing to the world. It is through these changes, apparently without order, and to the mind of childhood and ignorance, meaningless, that the machinery of the universe moves on, that the seasons do their appointed work, and seed-time and harvest bless the earth. These changes symbolize the movements of God's providence in the moral and social world. As through the changes in the physical world, the sunlight and dew, the darkness and storm, the oak puts on its sturdy growth of a hundred years, and the lily and rose gather in their sweetness and beauty of form and tint, so in the trials and struggles that come upon the children of men, does God build up human characters with strength to battle in days of conflict, with symmetry and beauty of development, a blessing to the world. But there is in human character, a possible grandeur, beauty and effectiveness which all the products of the natural world fail to symbolize. Man is in the image of God ; and though capable of culture and improvement like the lower forms of life, he has power to go forth as an independent actor, to understand the plans and purposes of creation, and to become, in promoting the progress and exaltation of mankind, a co-worker with God.

As an agency in bringing this world to its true place, back to its allegiance to Himself, and to aid in giving the knowledge of immortality and blessedness to all the race, God has established the church. Abraham was called, Christ came in the flesh and finally left that commission with his disciples, under which to-day ministers and missionaries offer the Gospel of reconciliation to those in the bondage and degradation of sin. Amid the darkness and gloom and hopelessness that rest upon the nations, there comes a light ; to those in the bondage of sin, a voice of promise comes from the servants of God, proclaiming pardon to captives, salvation to all nations, and the triumph of that everlasting kingdom of peace, which Christ came to establish.

What language more beautiful, what more appropriate to apply to the faithful and successful minister of the Gospel of Christ, than the words of the prophet (Isaiah lii : 7) : " How BEAUTIFUL UPON THE MOUNTAINS ARE THE FEET OF HIM THAT BRINGETH GOOD TIDINGS, THAT PUBLISHETH PEACE ; THAT BRINGETH GOOD TIDINGS OF GOOD, THAT PUBLISHETH SALVATION ; THAT SAITH UNTO ZION, THY GOD REIGNETH ! "

Such was the language most naturally suggested to my mind, when the telegraph announced to me that Dr. Gale was no more. His whole life, as I have known it for twenty-five years, his beautiful Christian character, his great success in the ministerial office, all came to view in a moment, and there seemed a beauty to gather around him as though revealed to my view amid the glories and triumphs that await those who have fought the good fight and finished their course. With the beauty of such a life, no emblem in the

physical earth or heavens can compare. The
light that comes from the character and teachings of such a man is more blessed and glorious than the light from star or planet, and it
will shine on when the sun shall fail and the
visible heavens shall pass away. It is the
lesson of such a life, its beauty and worth, that
I would gladly impress upon my own mind,
and that I would present to you, my friends,
not only for your comfort, but for our encouragement, guidance and profit, in what remains
to us of earthly work.

NAHUM GALE was born in Auburn, Mass.,
March 6, 1812, and united with the Congregational church in Worcester at the age of 18,
graduated at Amherst College in 1837, and at
the East Windsor Theological Seminary of
Connecticut in 1841. The following year,
June 22, 1842, he was ordained to the work
of the Gospel ministry. For more than thirty-
four years he has served the Master in the
church, and Theological Seminary, and in all
the varied duties and trusts that come upon
such a man in the promotion of education,
morals and religion among his own people
and in the world at large. The nature and

value of this work we can but briefly present, as we attempt an outline of that character which has grown in strength and beauty as the years have passed, a character that is a comfort to those who mourn and a blessing to the world.

The short record of dates and places that mark the history of his life is soon read; but the work of preparation, the labor and growth in the work of the ministry, the varied results of these long years of faithful labor will be known in their fullness only when the great white throne is set, and the books are opened. But so much is known to all those who have lived and labored with Dr. Gale, that his life must impress them as one of great beauty in its singleness of purpose, devotion and fitness for the pastoral work. The life of Dr. Gale was beautiful in its ordinary social relations. He had his share of trials and sorrow, but to him the world was no place for gloom and complaining. Where he moved, there was light and joy and enjoyment. A lover of the beautiful in Nature, a sympathizer with youth, he was welcome in all places as one who could rightly enjoy the world and teach others the

secret of that cheerfulness which may abound
with Christian love and zeal. As a choice
companion, Dr. Gale will ever be lovingly remembered by those who have had the good
fortune to be often associated with him. This
healthful social nature gave him access to men,
influence over the young, and made his daily
life a blessing to himself, and a source of enjoyment to all his friends. There was with
him ever a genial atmosphere, that won the
heart, and a manner that gave an air of at-
tractiveness and a new value to the common
duties of life as he performed them. There
was a deeper beauty still, known to those who
saw him in the family, in all those tender relations of which we may not speak even at such
a time as this, because their precious memories
belong to those who are called to weep, and
who will henceforth treasure them as a rich
legacy left by him to those dearest to his
heart. But there was another form of friendship in which the life of ˉour brother was a joy
and comfort to many beyond the range of his
family or kindred. I may be allowed to speak
of that kindness and helpfulness which he has
given to me in all the changes and responsi-

bilities of my official life.   Well can I adopt the
language of David in his bereavement, " Very
pleasant hast thou been unto me," my brother.

From the time that we first counseled together at East Windsor until he spoke his last
words of cheer and encouragement to me on
the stage at our last Commencement, he has
been to me an elder brother, in sound counsel,
in confidence and support.   The college has
lost one long faithful to her interests—faithful
and true in ways that the world knows little
of.   While the college has lost a wise counselor, an honored Trustee, I have lost a friend;
and my burden will be heavier, while I am
spared to active work, for this loss of one upon
whom I so much leaned, one who knew how,
and was prompt to speak kind words and do
kind and brave acts, at the right time.   Those
who saw Dr. Gale only in the common intercourse of life, where his genial companionship
was chiefly apparent, have little conception of
that caution and kindness and wisdom and
bravery that marked his action where principle
was involved and the right was to be main-
tained.

He was no mere fair-weather friend, no one

to float with the current when that current was against his convictions of truth and right. He would not willingly wound, but he would stand firm as a friend to truth though it put him in antagonism with those whom he loved and respected. Fortunate is it for an Institution to have such a man among its counselors and guardians, fortunate is the man who has such a one. for a friend in time of trial or of doubt. Of all these good qualities as adviser and friend, I have had abundant experience. His words and letters will still remain to me not only as tokens of his friendship, but as wise counselors still in the guidance of the college. The last words he spoke to me, were such as his heart would have prompted had he known he was giving me his last message—they were such as I shall ever remember with love for the man and encouragement in my work.

But the crowning beauty of the life of Dr. Gale, was his character and work as a Christian minister. This work was his choice ; to it he gave time and strength, yea his life, and to it all other purposes and pursuits in life were subordinate. It is this work which permeates and envelops all other forms of his activity, so that in whatever character we contemplate him, the Christian minister is the chief figure which attracts our attention. The testimony of his brethren and the abundant fruits which he gathered, to-day witness to his faithfulness and zeal and success in the pastoral office.

He began his work as settled pastor in Ware, where after a ministry of nine years, in which he endeared himself to his people and gained a good report among the brethren, he was called to the Professorship of Ecclesiastical History and Pastoral Duties in the Theological Institute of Connecticut, at East Windsor Hill. Though well fitted for this work and successful as an instructor, he felt drawn again to the more congenial work of the pastorate. From the Seminary, he came to this people. Why should I stand here to recount, to you, the people of his charge, his abundant labors for nearly a quarter of a century? Many who welcomed him as the new pastor here are gone. He has entered here many houses of mourning with the consolations of the Gospel. The children of that time now bear the burden and heat of the day. Those whom he baptized in infancy, as children of the church, have entered upon the active duties of life in this and other places. As the tidings of his death go out to other States, many eyes will grow dim at the remembrance of the beloved pastor who gave them counsel and comfort and led them to Him who could save. A great multitude of the living will remember him as their spiritual father—a great multitude on the heavenly shores, we believe, will welcome him to that blessedness which they have inherited through his faithful, loving ministrations. His brethren in the ministry will remember his sympathy and counsel; they will be encouraged in their work by his example, and, for long years, his name among them will be held in precious remembrance. The lesson of such a life is too valuable to be lost, and too varied to be presented in this short discourse. We should fail in our duty—we should lose what he would most desire for us, were he with us once more —were we to fail to gain instruction in the great work of the Christian life, from the example he has left us.

The first element of his success as a minister was in his thorough Christian character. No man was more deeply grounded in the

great doctrines of the Bible, known as evan-
gelical, than he.　He believed in the Bible,
and he believed that the Bible taught its truths
with fullness and plainness.　There was to him
also a Christian experience that bore witness
to the truths he preached.　He warned men
to flee from the wrath to come.　He pointed
them to a Saviour able to save all, even to the
uttermost, of those who come to God by Him.
It was thus—his intellectual apprehension of
the scheme of salvation and his own religious
experience harmonizing—that there was with
him no waste of strength, no doubt and no
holding back.　Body, mind and spirit moved
in unison in the great work in which he was
engaged.　It was thus that he became a power;
it was thus, with this intellectual and emotional
basis for action, that he has brought this re-
markable pastorate to a close, only with the
close of his life.　And the last words which he
spoke were a fitting close to such a ministry
and such a Christian life.　" *All my trust is
in the Saviour I have preached so long.　I trust
Him wholly.　The doctrines I have preached
I believe are true, true now and true forever.　I rest on them.*"　Dr. Gale by nature

had certain qualifications that fitted him in an unusual degree for the pastoral office. He was naturally alive to the interests of all people wherever he moved. He was genial and sympathetic, so that his company was cheerful to the aged and attractive to the young. And this natural suavity of temper was blended with that religious principle and sense of duty that kept him in sympathy with his people and the work of the kingdom to the last.

Another ground of success was devotion to his work. How abundant in labors he was, how cheerfully and gladly he bore every burden that belongs to the Christian ministry! He was not only the oldest settled pastor in the Congregational churches of the county, but he was also the senior pastor among all the denominations. Of those who assisted at his installation only three are now living.

At no time, in all his ministry, was he dearer to his people, the old and the young, than in the last year of his life. The labor required to lead such a people, as a faithful shepherd, for so many years, could be performed only by one who loved the work in which he was engaged. Of his most abundant labors no

earthly record could be made; but the in-
gathering into this church and the impulse that
he gave to the Gospel work beyond the bounds
of his own parish, witness to his devotion to
his Master's cause.   His last earthly labor, on
the Saturday before his death, was dictating a
letter in reference to the Home Missionary
work.

And now that his labor is done, and we re-
view that work, that life given to the service of
God in the holy ministry, what other office
seems so grand as the pastoral office?   Who
among the nobles of earth can compare with
him who has finished such a life, falling in the
midst of his work and yet having done a work
that might have been counted complete at any
moment that the Master called.   In this hour
of our bereavement and sadness, there beams
forth a light that gives joy to every mourning
heart.   The world is brighter and better for
such a life ; it seems like another star set in the
spiritual firmament to give new glory to the
heavens and light to the earth.

 " *How beautiful upon the mountains are the
feet of him that bringeth good tidings ; that publisheth peace ; that bringeth good tidings of good,*

*that publisheth salvation ; that saith unto Zion,
Thy God reigneth !* "

And how beautiful, thou servant of God,
among the redeemed with the palm of victory,
wearing the crown of rejoicing, that crown of
glory whose brightness and stars are but symbols of souls redeemed through thy ministrations !

But the " field is the world," and precious
seed must still be sown. There are battles still
to be fought under the banners of the Gospel,
and though one soldier after another puts off
his armor and passes to his reward, others must
press forward into the vacant places, hold the
ground already won, and march on to new con-
quests, till the triumph of the Redeemer's kingdom is complete. We have something more
to do to-day than to recount the virtues and
rejoice in the victory of him who has been
called from his work. It becomes us to inquire
what new duty this dispensation brings to us
who remain. One of the fathers of the churches
has fallen, one of the oldest and most honored
pastors of the county has stepped from his place,
to return no more. His pulpit, his place in the
councils of the church, in the missionary work,

in the college, and all those labors in which he
was so abundant, are to be filled by others, or
the cause of the kingdom must suffer loss. To
you, his brethren in the ministry, he speaks
to-day, speaks by the work he has done, by the
places once filled by him, now vacant. Though
not properly one of you in the office of the
ministry, I cannot forget the inroads made upon
your number in this county ; and as you are
called upon to bear this heavy loss, I would
cheer you by this example of a long and faithful pastorate, I would incite you to renewed
diligence and zeal by presenting anew the great
work in which you are engaged, and the great
need in our very midst, in our State, our nation,
and the world, of such Christian labors as this
people have long enjoyed. If this loss shall stir
the heart of every pastor in the county to new
faith and zeal and activity in his ministry, shall
kindle in each one new and deeper love for the
Gospel as the appointed means for the salvation
of men, this example will do its appropriate
work, this death will be blessed to the upbuilding of the churches that are now called to
mourn.

The voice comes not to ministers alone, but

to all the people of our county. The fathers
of the churches are passing away or bending
under the weight of years. There are vacant
pulpits, there are churches that need new life
and power. The time has come for every
member of the church of Christ to hold himself a worker in the vineyard of the Lord. Let
the pastors accept the new responsibilities, let
all the people offer themselves willingly as
of old, to the service of God, and our county, beautiful in its mountain, stream and valley, shall become more beautiful in its living
churches, in its people honoring God and de-
lighting in his service.

To the family and people what words can
come freighted with the comfort and consolation which you crave ? What more can be
done, than to recount the closing scenes of his
triumphant death, to recall the words of tender-
ness and love as he remembered his people,
the people that he loved, and in whose love he
had perfect trust ? " Deal tenderly with me
now," said he, " it is the day of my disappointment," when he found he was to meet his people no more on earth. " Tell the people how
I have loved them." But, though longing to see

you once more, though his thoughts were busy with new plans for the instruction of the young, though he might, according to the ordinary course of life. look forward to years of active labor and a fuller realization of his plans, yet his language was, as death approached, " It is all right, all right." And thus with many loving words that may not be spoken here, with unshaken faith in Christ and hope of everlasting life, he passed to his rest. What sweeter consolation than this to the bereaved wife and children and to this mourning church'?

To the Heavenly Father who has blessed you with this beautiful life, to Him who afflicts not willingly, whose grace is abundant, whose mercy everlasting, I commend you. May the light of God's countenance never depart from one of the bereaved family, may the fires of holy love and Christian zeal glow brighter than ever upon the altar of this church. May this new name, added to that other long remembered and honored here, be cherished by all this people as a new example of faithfulness, ever recalling the precious seasons of the past, and inciting them towards that land of peace and rest, where pastor and people shall rejoice together, where there shall be no more death, where they shall together worship in that city, where the Lord God Almighty and the Lamb are the temple of it.   Amen.

3*

REV. DR. GRIFFIN.

"THE RIGHTEOUS HATH HOPE IN HIS DEATH."
How different are these words from the natural language of this world! The wisdom of this world sees hope in the plans and purposes of life, disappointment and dread in all that pertains to death.

At such a time as this, we all need that light and support which God is ever offering to us in his revealed Word. It is a light and guide to us through all this earthly pilgrimage—a pillar of cloud by day, and a pillar of fire by night. But it is in the days of darkness and sorrow that its preciousness is most clearly revealed. When we are in the midst of prosperity, when no sorrow is upon us, we are prone to forget the precious promises here made for the comfort and support of the children of God. But when affliction comes upon us, these promises shine forth as stars gather in the evening sky when the light of day

grows dim, until the whole concave is gleam-
ing with shining worlds.

It is not strange that the Bible, as a whole,
is opposed in its teachings to the maxims of
the world. The Bible is the word of God and
contains His holy law, while man is in rebellion
against his God, by nature a sinful being, and
by practice a transgressor of that law. The
maxims of men have special reference to this
world; the Bible everywhere recognizes an
endless life. It lays hold on an eternal world.
Among these great truths peculiar to Revela-
tion, I have selected these words as appropriate
for our contemplation at this time.

" *The righteous hath hope in his death.*"
How opposed is this to the maxims of the men
of fashion, the ambitious, and the worldly-wise.
To them death is the end of all hope. Their
good is in this life, and their hope reaches on
towards earthly success and sensual gratifica-
tion. They must hurry on and grasp the prize
before death comes to blast their hopes forever.
But not so with the righteous. He may have
been among the humble and unknown, or
among the honored of earth, but the day of his
death is the day of brightest hope for him. As

he is ready to bid adieu to earth, he is permitted to indulge hopes unknown to other men.
His work is indeed done, but his God still
lives and rules upon the earth—his labors may
therefore yet be blessed after he has passed
away, his prayers for loved ones may yet be
answered by that covenant-keeping God, who
shows mercies to thousands of those who love
him and keep his commandments. He com-
mits the dear ones to the care of Him, who
is the Father of the fatherless and the God of
the bereaved.

But what shall I say of that hope which en-
ters into that within the vail ? That hope which
lays hold of the great promise of eternal life
and of eternal blessedness through Jesus Christ?
What a blessed hope ! a hope that death alone
made possible. Life was an imperfect arch ;
but now death, radiant with the hopes that
brighten in its presence, makes the arch perfect,
and the central hope of the soul is changed to
glad fruition.

Through death, the believer is freed from a
sinful body. In life there was a war in the
members, but now there is to be a joyful en-
trance into the company of the redeemed, where

sin, with all its allurements, is unknown, where we believe that he, whose death we mourn, now walks freed from the body of this death.

The believer has hope of the resurrection of the body. It may not be shadowed forth in nature, but it is revealed in the Bible. In the wreck of the universe not one of the dead shall be forgotten. At the peal of the trump of God, the dead in Christ shall rise first, they shall be caught up to meet their Lord in the air. Yea, more than this, though the heavens and the earth pass away, the inheritance of the saints of God shall remain sure, they shall enter the pearly gates, they shall stand upon the sea of glass mingled with fire ; they shall eat of the tree of life and drink of the river of water of life proceeding out of the throne of God and the Lamb. There shall be no more death, neither sorrow nor crying, for God himself shall be with them and wipe away all tears from their eyes.

Such was the hope of him who has now passed away. The power and beauty of a Christian life was manifest in all he did. For thirty years he has lived among this people, faithful to the college and to the church—faithful in all the

relations of life. His precepts and example
agreed. His trust in the Bible and the God of
the Bible was complete. If any one among us
was worthy of the name of theologian, Dr. Griffin
was the man. But in the simplicity and fullness
of his faith and trust, he was a Christian. And
the strength and beauty of his Christian character were clearly revealed as he came near the
end. When the outward man began to weaken,
the inward man, renewed day by day, put on
that strength which is the promise of immortality. He was the one to speak words of comfort and consolation. Trusting in Him who has
conquered death and the grave, his spirit rose
above the weakness of the body, so that his last
days will remain a pleasant remembrance to his
family and friends.

And now that still another to whom I looked
for words of advice and encouragement has
gone, I feel more than ever before alone, and
remember that the burdens of life must become
heavier as one after another falls, in whom I
have trusted for aid and support. But there is
still instruction and strength to be gained from
the example of the wise and good who are gone.
From the example of this life now closed, I

would fain gain profit for myself. And to his friends and neighbors, his life and death are full of instruction. It would not be in accordance with his own request for me to speak of him as my own heart might prompt me to speak. As I sat with him alone for the last time, it was pleasant to know that in the long years of our intercourse no shadow had fallen between us, that we could recall the past, which seemed clear as the vision of day in his thoughts, without words of explanation or regret. As he gave his last messages and requests, his words were : " If you can speak a word that shall profit the living, I shall be glad, but say little as possible of me " Nor need I speak words of him to those who can recall the example which he has left. His faithfulness in all the duties of life that devolved upon him, and his courage and submission, as this fatal disease made its inroads upon him, must be a stimulus to us in all our work, a new cause of faithfulness in that Christian life that brought so much consolation to him as the world was fading away.

And to you, my beloved friends, the bereaved wife and children, and all of you upon whom this loss falls so heavily, what words can I speak that shall give any comfort and consolation that you do not already possess, in the loving words and in the remembrance of the Christian life and glorious hope of him for whom we all mourn to-day?   I can but commend you to the Word of God. and to the blessings of His grace. May He sustain you in all your way, and enable us all to follow him who is gone as he followed the Divine Master, and bring us, through infinite grace in Jesus Christ, to that rest that remaineth to the people of God.   AMEN.

President Chadbourne's Works.

PUBLISHED BY

G. P. PUTNAM'S SONS,

182 Fifth Avenue,   *New York.*

I. NATURAL THEOLOGY, or Nature and the Bible, from the
same Author. 12mo, cloth, . . $1.50

II. INSTINCT IN ANIMALS AND MEN, 12mo, cloth, $1.75

III. THE HOPE OF THE RIGHTEOUS, 12mo. $

IV. THE STRENGTH OF MEN AND STABILITY OF NATIONS.
(In Press.)

www.ingramcontent.com/pod-product-compliance
Lightning Source LLC
Chambersburg PA
CBHW030854260626
47169CB00008B/2534